# What's New at the Zoo?

written by Judy Nayer
illustrated by Theresa Burns

Macmillan
McGraw-Hill

New York          Farmington

"What can we learn at the
zoo?" asked Chuck.

"Let's go together now!"
said Hank.

"Look! They swing from branch to branch!" said Chuck.

"They swing a lot!" said Hank.

"Look!" said Hank. "They swim and jump in the tank!"

"Lunch!" said Chuck.
"They eat fish for lunch!"

"Let's go on this ride!" said Hank.
"What is in the grass?"

"Big, big cats!" said Chuck.

"Big cats run fast!" said Hank.

"Look, Hank!" said Chuck.
"I can run fast, too!"